ATLANTIS
THE LOST EMPIRE

LEVEL 6

Re-told by: Marie Crook
Series Editor: Melanie Williams

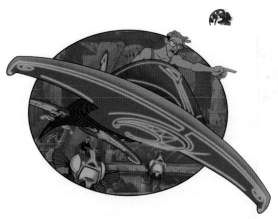

DISCARDED

Pearson Education Limited
Edinburgh Gate, Harlow,
Essex CM20 2JE, England
and Associated Companies throughout the world.

ISBN: 978-1-4082-8818-4

This edition first published by Pearson Education Ltd 2012

1 3 5 7 9 10 8 6 4 2

Text copyright © Pearson Education Ltd 2012
Copyright © 2012 Disney Enterprises, Inc. All rights reserved.

The moral rights of the author have been asserted
in accordance with the Copyright Designs and Patents Act 1988

Set in 15/19pt OT Fiendstar
Printed in China
SWTC/01

Published by Pearson Education Ltd in association with
Penguin Books Ltd, both companies being subsidiaries of Pearson Plc

For a complete list of the titles available in the Penguin Kids series please go to www.penguinreaders.com.
Alternatively, write to your local Pearson Longman office or to: Penguin Readers Marketing Department,
Pearson Education, Edinburgh Gate, Harlow, Essex CM20 2JE, England.

Thousands of years ago, the Empire of Atlantis was a wonderful place. The people of Atlantis were intelligent. They built computers, amazing buildings, and fantastic flying machines. Their lives were as comfortable as our lives are today.

Then one day, a terrible thing happened. A great storm came to Atlantis. The sky became dark and the ocean became angry. The waters rose higher and higher, and soon they covered everything and everyone. In just one day, the whole Empire of Atlantis disappeared.

Milo Thatch loved hearing his grandfather's stories about the lost Empire of Atlantis. His grandfather told these stories every night when Milo was young. Milo was excited by this wonderful place. His grandfather always said, "Remember, Milo, Atlantis was a real place. Maybe you'll find it one day."

Then, sadly, Milo's grandfather died. When Milo grew up, he became a teacher. He dreamed of finding Atlantis one day, but he had no money, no time, and no one to help him.

Milo did not think that his dream would come true.

Milo imagined Atlantis and he read about Atlantis. He studied Atlantis and taught his students everything he knew about Atlantis. Many did not believe his stories. Was Atlantis a real place? How could there be flying machines and computers thousands of years ago?

"The stories are true," Milo told his students, again and again. "You have to believe me! Atlantis was a real place!"

Then, suddenly one evening, everything changed for Milo Thatch.

Milo returned home from work and found a strange woman in his house. "Are you Milo Thatch?" she asked. "There's a very important man who would like to meet you. His name's Mr. Whitmore. Come with me."

Milo was a little scared, but he always liked an adventure. He followed the woman to Mr. Whitmore's house.

Mr. Whitmore was waiting for them in front of the fire. He smiled when he saw Milo. "I knew your grandfather very well," said Mr. Whitmore. "He gave me this package before he died. He asked me to give it to you."

Milo smiled sadly. He missed his grandfather so much and now he had a gift from him. He opened the package carefully. It was a book. The language was not English. It was Atlantian.

Mr. Whitmore said, "This is a very important book, Milo, and I know that you can understand it. You'll learn all the secrets of Atlantis from this book. It will help you to find the lost Empire."

"Wow!" breathed Milo. "I'll leave America tomorrow! I'll take a little boat ..."

"Wait!" said Mr. Whitmore. "Forget the little boat. I have something much better for you."

Mr. Whitmore took Milo to a window. Milo saw a big room. There was a small submarine in it.

"Her name's Ulysses and she's all yours," said Mr. Whitmore. "I have a lot of money and I would like to help you."

Mr. Whitmore explained his promise to Milo's grandfather. "I told him that I'd help you to find Atlantis. Your grandfather was a good friend and a great man."

"So, Atlantis is waiting!" cried Mr. Whitmore. "What do you say?"

"I'm your man," smiled Milo. "When can we leave?"

Milo started to feel a little nervous when he climbed on to the real submarine. He loved an adventure, but he was only a teacher.

He did not have to worry. Everything he needed was already on the submarine.

There was a crew of 200 people to help Milo with his adventure. Milo would not be alone and he would have a lot of help.

Then he met Commander Rourke, a big, strong, friendly man. Milo liked Commander Rourke. "Wow! We're leaving America! We're going to find Atlantis!"

Milo spoke to his crew. "It will be difficult to reach Atlantis. A sea monster guards the entrance to the Empire. But if we get there, it will be wonderful!" he said.

"The Atlantians had everything we have today," he explained, "like computers and flying machines."

"Impossible!" said one of the crew. "What did they use for power?"

"In my book, it says that they used crystals," said Milo, "but I need to read more."

The crew listened, but they did not believe Milo's stories. They laughed at Milo.

Suddenly, they heard a terrible noise.

Milo stopped talking and Commander Rourke turned on the lights. They felt something hit the submarine. It shot past the windows and Milo noticed its long, thick tail.

"Wham!" it hit them again. It was a machine sea monster.

Commander Rourke and the crew acted immediately.

"Shoot it!" Rourke cried, "... and kill it!"

The sea monster was strong and the fight was long and hard.

When the monster was dead they came to land. Everyone looked around. They were in trouble. Many of the crew were dead.

Commander Rourke looked at the submarine. "We can't use this again," he said, "but we must continue. Can you drive a truck, Milo?"

Milo was scared. This was not a fun adventure. The sea monster was fierce. Lots of people were already dead. And now Commander Rourke was asking him to drive a big truck!

But Milo drove the truck and after some time, the crew decided to stop and camp for the night.

Milo could not put up his tent.

The crew laughed at Milo. "Does he belong here?" one asked.

"I don't believe his stories!" said another. "He knows nothing!"

"But Milo was right about the sea monster," another said, "and he fought well."

Then the crew invited Milo to sit with them. They talked for hours about everything. Everyone in the crew was different and knew different things.

"We're a good team," said Milo, "because we're all different."

Later, Milo was reading his book when he noticed a missing page. It was the page about the crystal power on Atlantis – a very important page.

That night, the crew climbed into their tents and slept. But when Milo heard a noise, he crawled out of his tent.

He saw lots of small, bright lights. They were coming toward him and there were thousands of them. Milo cried out when he noticed everything they touched turned to fire. They were fireflies!

"Fire!" cried Milo, and he ran.

The crew woke up. They tried to escape the fireflies in their trucks. But the trucks were on fire and they fell off a bridge. When the crew came to a stop they noticed Milo was not with them.

Milo was lying on the ground and he was hurt. When he opened his eyes he jumped. A person in a big mask was looking at him closely. Milo was afraid. A hand slowly pulled up the mask. Milo could see a very beautiful woman.

The woman took a crystal from around her neck and touched Milo's chest with it. The crystal made him better.

Then she quickly turned and ran away.

"Wait!" cried Milo. "Who are you?"

Milo was looking for the woman when he saw the crew on top of a hill. "We were looking for you," they said, "but guess what we found!" They pointed and Milo looked over the hill. He could not believe his eyes. "Atlantis!" he cried. "We're here!"

A group of people in masks suddenly jumped out in front of them. Milo was not afraid. "These must be the Atlantians," he said.

"What?" asked one of the crew. "Isn't that impossible? Didn't the Atlantian people all die thousands of years ago?"

"In Atlantis, nothing is impossible," smiled Milo.

The Atlantians took off their masks and Milo saw the beautiful woman. He knew some Atlantian language from his book. He tried to speak to her and was very surprised when the woman replied in English. She explained that the Atlantians knew lots of languages.

"Welcome to Atlantis! My name's Kida," she said. "We're glad you are here. Atlantis is in trouble. We've lost the 'Heart of Atlantis'. It's our most powerful crystal. Without it, Atlantis will soon die."

"I hope that you can help us," she said.

Kida took Milo and the crew to meet her father, the Emperor.
He was an old, old man and he was very sick. He was not
pleased to see them.

"You must leave Atlantis immediately," said the Emperor.
"You don't belong here and we don't need your help."

"We've lived well for thousands of years," he continued. "Believe
me, Kida, we don't need these people."

"Can we stay for one more night?" Commander Rourke
asked the Emperor. "We've come a long way and we
need to rest now."

The Emperor agreed.

When the crew left to put up their tents, Kida spoke to her father. She felt very unhappy and a little angry. "My opinion is different from yours," she explained. "We need to find the Heart of Atlantis and maybe these people can help."

"We can learn nothing from them," said her father.

Kida did not want to fight with her father, so she kissed him and left sadly.

Then Kida went to find Milo.

Kida told Milo about the Atlantians' problems and Milo told her about the book his grandfather gave to him. "I can't read Atlantian," Kida said, "but I think this book can help us."

Milo agreed. "We'll work together," he said.

Kida showed Milo an old flying machine and explained that she could not make it work.

"I don't understand how to mend it," she said.

Milo read his book, then tried to mend it himself. He used the crystal from around Kida's neck. Suddenly, the machine jumped back into life!

Kida took Milo to the highest place in the Empire and showed him the whole of Atlantis. When he looked at it, Milo thought about his grandfather. He wanted to cry.

Kida liked Milo. She knew he loved Atlantis and wanted to help.

That night, Kida and Milo talked about Atlantis and its future. "There's a painting in a cave," she said. "I think it's important, but I don't understand it."

"Maybe the book can help us," said Milo. "Let's go there now."

The painting was underwater. They had to swim to it.

Milo felt shy. He liked Kida a lot.

They jumped into the pool. Milo was excited when they reached the painting. "It shows the whole history of Atlantis!" he said.

"Does it tell us where to find the Heart of Atlantis?" asked Kida.

Milo swam down to the bottom of the pool and looked at the painting. "Wow!" he cried when he came up. "You're not going to believe what's down there!"

"The Heart of Atlantis is somewhere under here!" Milo said. "That's what the painting says!"

"Wow!" said Kida. "We found it! But how do we reach it?"

Milo was not sure. He thought he could find the information in his book, but then he remembered the missing page. It worried him. Why would someone take a page from his book? He was sure that it was the most important page, the page which would lead them to the Heart of Atlantis.

Milo swam to the top of the pool. He jumped with surprise when he saw Commander Rourke and the crew. They looked unhappy. They looked different ... and they had guns.

Commander Rourke was holding the missing page of Milo's book. "Are you looking for this?" asked Rourke. "Thank you for finding the Heart of Atlantis. Now tell me how to get it!"

Suddenly, Milo understood. Rourke and the crew were not good people. They were the enemy! They did not want to save Atlantis. They wanted to steal its power for themselves.

Milo and Kida climbed out of the water. One of the crew quickly caught Kida and held her.

"The crystal isn't treasure that you can sell for money!" explained Milo. "Without it, the people of Atlantis will die!"

Commander Rourke laughed. "You say it isn't treasure," he said, "but if we take that crystal back to America, we'll become rich!"

The crew asked Milo to help them. "Why don't you join us, Milo? You'll be rich, too!"

When Milo refused, Rourke said, "Ha! I knew it! You're too nice ... just like your grandfather."

Commander Rourke showed Milo the missing page. I must not lead these people to the Heart of Atlantis, Milo decided.

"The Heart of Atlantis lies in the eyes of the Emperor," he read. What could that mean? The eyes of the Emperor ... .

Then Milo saw the Emperor. He was watching them from behind a rock. Commander Rourke hit him and he fell. When the Emperor looked up, his eyes looked like a mirror. In them, Milo could see where the Heart of Atlantis lay, under the water. Rourke saw it, too.

Commander Rourke jumped into the water and Milo and the crew followed. The crew were angry with Rourke because he hit the Emperor. They knew that this was wrong.

They reached the place in the water that they saw in the Emperor's eyes. A door opened under their feet. They dropped down into a cave. There was a large crystal shining in the air above their heads.

"The Heart of Atlantis," breathed Kida. The crystal around her neck was moving.

The Heart of Atlantis was pulling Kida toward it with its power and light.

Soon Milo and the crew could not see Kida. She was inside the Heart of Atlantis. They waited and watched, afraid. Then, very slowly, Kida started to come back down to the ground. She looked like a crystal! She was full of light. She walked slowly toward Milo.

Suddenly, Commander Rourke caught Kida and put her in a large box. He locked the box and threw it in his truck.

"Now we have our treasure!" he laughed. "We have the Heart of Atlantis and the girl! What a result!"

Milo screamed at Commander Rourke. "You're killing the Empire of Atlantis! Why would you do that? For money? Because you want to be famous?"

Rourke turned and hit Milo in the face. Milo fell to the ground. A picture of Milo and his grandfather fell out of his bag. Rourke smiled. "It's time to go!" he said to the crew.

Some of the crew looked at Rourke and then at Milo. "This is wrong and you know it!" they said to Rourke. They walked away from Rourke and toward Milo. "We are joining you, Milo," they said. "We want to help you."

Commander Rourke jumped in his truck and drove angrily away with his friends. Kida was in the box in the back of the truck.

Milo and the crew decided to go to the Emperor. They explained about the large crystal and Kida.

"The Heart of Atlantis is inside Kida now," said the Emperor. "That's why she was full of light."

"You need to find her and return the Heart of Atlantis to the right place," he said. "If you can do this, you'll save Kida and you'll save Atlantis."

The Emperor gave Milo a small crystal. "This will help you," he said.

After speaking to the Emperor, Milo was scared. "I can't do this," he said. "I'm only a teacher! I can't save the Empire of Atlantis!"
The crew told Milo to remember his brave grandfather. Now Milo had to be brave, too.

Milo listened. He knew that they were right. He was a different man now. He *was* a braver man and he could save Atlantis. He wanted to make his grandfather proud.

The crew wanted to help Milo. "There are some flying machines here," they said, "but they're all old and they don't move."

Milo saw the flying machine when he was with Kida. Then he remembered the crystal that the Emperor gave him. "I can mend these," he said. "I've learned a lot!"

Soon the machines were ready to go. Milo and the crew jumped into the flying machines and flew toward the gates of Atlantis. They saw Commander Rourke in his truck, but he was not alone.

He was with friends and they had guns!

Commander Rourke and his friends started shooting at Milo and the crew when they saw them. There was fire everywhere. The crew flew fast and fought bravely.

Milo moved closer to Rourke and his truck. When he reached him, Rourke laughed at Milo. "Do you think that you are brave, little man?" Rourke asked.

Commander Rourke was much bigger than Milo and Milo suddenly did not feel brave.

Then he thought about his grandfather and Kida and the Empire of Atlantis. He came toward Rourke angrily and cut him with a crystal.

Commander Rourke screamed when he died.

Milo used a flying machine to pull the box with Kida inside. He took it to the cave under the water. Then he used his crystal to open the box.

As soon as the box opened, the cave filled with light. Kida was standing there. She was shining like the sun.

Kida slowly turned around and around and then she started to rise up toward the sky. The Heart of Atlantis left her body and returned to its home.

Suddenly, Kida began to fall. Milo ran and caught her in his arms. Kida looked into Milo's eyes and smiled.

"Thank you, Milo," she said. "You saved my life and you saved Atlantis."

Milo thought Kida was very beautiful. He loved Kida very much and she loved him, too.

Milo and Kida looked around them. The Empire of Atlantis looked wonderful. They knew that the Heart was in the right place now.

Everything would be okay again and Kida's father would be so grateful.

Milo decided to stay in Atlantis.

The crew joined Milo and Kida. "My friends helped me a lot!" said Milo, smiling.

"We chose the right team," said the crew. "We're glad we helped you. Atlantis is more important than money."

Milo told the crew that he did not want to return to his old life.
He would stay with Kida in Atlantis now.

"Are you sure you want to stay?" they asked. "America will welcome you back with open arms! You are the man who discovered Atlantis!"

"I'm sure," said Milo. "This is my home now."

The crew began the long journey back to America. "What shall we tell Mr. Whitmore?" they asked themselves.

"We can't tell him the truth. We can't tell him that we wanted to steal the Heart of Atlantis ..."

"Whitmore doesn't need to know," said one. "We did the right thing in the end."

"And the world doesn't need to know about Atlantis," said another. "The Atlantians don't need any more trouble."

When they arrived in America, they had a story for Mr. Whitmore.

"Milo Thatch died when a sea monster attacked Ulysses on the journey to Atlantis," one of the crew told Mr. Whitmore. "We couldn't find Atlantis without him, so we decided to come home."

They did not want to lie to the kind Mr. Whitmore, but it was necessary. Mr. Whitmore was sad, but he was also glad. Milo fought for his dream. He was a brave man.

Of course, the crew could not forget Atlantis or their brave friend Milo, whose dream came true because he fought for it.

Before You Read

❶ Match the words and pictures.

Emperor
submarine
crystal
book
truck
fireflies

❷ Look at the picture on the cover and describe what you can see. Say what you think will happen in this story.

After You Read

❶ Which of these things can you find in the story of *Atlantis: The Lost Empire*?

Kida	a robot	a submarine
Milo	a police officer	a book
a crew	an Empire	a zoo
a sea monster	a dolphin	a crystal
some treasure	some chocolate	a mask

Activity page ❷

❷ Read and write True (T) or False (F).

a Thousands of years ago, Atlantis had computers.

b Mr. Whitmore gave Milo a book and a submarine.

c Commander Rourke was a very good man and a great friend.

d Milo doesn't learn anything on his journey to Atlantis.

e The Heart of Atlantis is a large restaurant.

f Commander Rourke takes the Heart of Atlantis back to Mr. Whitmore.

g Milo saves Kida and the Empire of Atlantis.

h When the crew return to America, they tell Mr. Whitmore the truth.

❸ On page 24, Milo learns that Commander Rourke is not a good person. Why? Tell your friend.

❹ Answer the questions.

a What was Atlantis like thousands of years ago?

b What was Milo's job?

c Why did Mr. Whitmore want to help Milo?

d Who went with Milo on his journey to Atlantis?

e Many of the submarine crew died. Why? What happened?

f Who did Milo meet in Atlantis?

g What happened next in the story?